John S. Ogilvie

The Album Writer's Friend

Comprising more than three hundred choice selections of poetry and

prose, suitable for writing in autograph albums, valentines, birthday,

Christmas and New Year cards

John S. Ogilvie

The Album Writer's Friend
Comprising more than three hundred choice selections of poetry and prose, suitable for writing in autograph albums, valentines, birthday, Christmas and New Year cards

ISBN/EAN: 9783337259891

Printed in Europe, USA, Canada, Australia, Japan

Cover: Foto ©Andreas Hilbeck / pixelio.de

More available books at **www.hansebooks.com**

THE
ALBUM WRITER'S FRIEND.

COMPRISING MORE THAN

THREE HUNDRED CHOICE SELECTIONS OF POETRY AND PROSE,

SUITABLE FOR WRITING IN AUTOGRAPH ALBUMS, VALEN-
TINES, BIRTHDAY, CHRISTMAS AND NEW YEAR CARDS.

ORIGINAL AND SELECTED.

Our lives are albums, written through
With good or ill, with false or true,
And as the blessed angels turn the pages **of our** years,
God grant that they **may** read **the** good with smiles,
And blot the ill with tears.

COMPILED BY J. S. OGILVIE.

NEW YORK:
J. S. OGILVIE AND COMPANY,
25 Rose Street.

PREFACE.

WHO among the readers of this preface has not been invited to write a few words of sentiment in the Album of a friend? As an aid to the many thousands who have received this invitation, and have not known **what to write, we** offer this collection of choice verse and prose, **as an aid to** them and all others, **with** the hope that our labor shall not have been **spent in** vain, nor be altogether **unappreciated.** Great care **has** been taken to procure as many *original pieces* as **possible.** Many choice verses suitable for Birthday, Christmas and New-Year celebrations, have been added; **which,** with the collection of **articles embracing sentiment,** affection, humor, and **miscellany,** is **offered to** a generous public by

THE COMPILER.

CONTENTS.

>—DEDICATION VERSES—<

> Go forth, thou little volume,
>   Like Noah's faithful dove,
> And bring to darling ———
>   An olive leaf of love.

> My Album's **open! Come and see!**
> What! **Won't you waste a line** on me?
> Write but **a** thought, a word or two,
> **That** Memory may revert to you.

To My Friends:—

> My Album is a garden spot
>   Where **all** my friends **may sow,**
> Where thorns and thistles flourish not,
>   But flowers alone may grow.
> With smiles for sunshine, tears for showers,
> I'll water, watch and guard these flowers.

5

Go forth, thou little volume,
I leave thee to thy fate ;
To love and friendship truly
Thy leaves I dedicate.

Go, Album! range the gay parterre;
From gem to gem, from flower to flower,
Select with taste and cull with care,
And bring your offering, fresh and rare,
To this sweet maiden's bower!

When years elapse,
It may, perhaps,
Delight us to review these scraps,
And live again 'mid scenes so gay,
That Time's rough hand has swept away;
For when the eye, bedimmed with age,
Shall rest upon each treasured page,
Those pleasant hours
That once were ours
Shall come again, like Autumn flowers,
To bloom and smile upon us here
When all things else seem sad and drear;
'Twill tune our hearts and make them sing,
And turn our Autumn into Spring!

Go, little book, thy destined course pursue,
Collect memorials of the just and true,
And beg of every friend so near
Some token of remembrance dear.

As life flows on from day to day,
And this, your book, soon fills,
How many may be far away
From treasured vales and hills?

But there is joy in future time
To turn the pages o'er,
And see within a name or rhyme
From one you'll see no more.

———

LIFE is a volume,
From youth to old age,
Each year forms a chapter,
Each day is a page.
May none be more charming,
More womanly (manly) true,
Than that, pure and noble,
Sketched yearly by you.

———

Many kind wishes will be written here,
And none more sincere than mine.
But——
Words are lighter than the cloud-foam
Of the restless ocean's spray;
Vainer than the trembling shadow
That the next hour steals away:
By the fall of summer raindrops
Is the air as deeply stirred,
And the roseleaf that we tread on
Will outlive a word.

WE may write our names in Albums;
We may trace them in the sand;
We may chisel them in marble,
With a firm and skillful hand:
But the pages soon are sullied,
Soon each name will fade away;
Every monument will crumble,
Like all earthy hopes, decay.
But, dear friend, there is an Album,
Full of leaves of snowy white,
Where no name is ever tarnished,
But forever pure and bright.
In that Book of Life, God's Album,
May your name be penned with care,
And may all who here may write,
Have their names forever there.

SENTIMENT and AFFECTION.

PEACE be around thee, wherever thou rovest;
  May life be for thee one summer's day;
And all that thou wish, and all that thou **lovest,**
  Come smiling around **thy** summer way.
If sorrow e'er this calm should break,
  May even thy tears pass off so lightly,
Like spring showers, they will **only make**
  The smiles that follow shine more **brightly.**

MAY the chain of friendship formed by the links which are dropped here, serve **to** unite you more closely in spirit with the friends who **have** worked it.

May each link be brought **to** a white heat **in** the fires of Love; **and, forged on** the anvils of **Truth, may** they be strong **as iron, yet light as air:** keeping you bravely to the duties **of Life. And when the chain of** human bondage shall **be** broken, **may they become** flowers of eternal brightness in the gardens from whence cometh exceeding peace.

OUR lives are albums, written **through**
With good or ill—with **false or true—**
And, **as** the blessed **angels turn**
The pages of our years,
God grant they read **the** good with smiles,
  And blot the **bad with tears.**

9

THE gem cannot be polished without friction, nor man perfected without adversity.

TIME advances like the slowest tide, but retreats like the swiftest current.

WHAT'S the use of always fretting
    At the trials we shall find
Ever strewn along our pathway—
    Travel on, and never mind.

LIFE giveth unto each his space,
    A span of earth, an arch of sky,
And unto each a several grace—
    To each a separate destiny.
And some were born to win and spend,
And some to love unto the end.

THERE is another album
Filled with leaves of spotless white,
    Where no name is ever tarnished,
But forever pure and bright.
    In the Book of Life—God's album—
May your name be penned with care,
    And may all who here have written,
Write their names forever there.

DAILY we write our autographs on the minds and hearts of those around us.

"Poor is the friendless master of **a world.** A world
in purchase for a friend, is gain."

———————

So slight **a favor 'tis** you crave,
    That I can scarce refuse compliance;
Nor shall **I** use the page you gave,
    To set your champions at defiance.

Dear lady, vainly awed, I praise
    That dimpled hand I pressed **at parting;**
Or those dark **eyes,** beneath whose **gaze**
    A cupid lurks equipped for **darting.**

Nor can **I** hope **to lightly touch**
    On charms **so** oft the **theme of lovers;**
To add **another,** while so **much**
    That **beautiful about thee** hovers.

I can but add one little pearl
    To all the gems about thee scattered;
And say again, sweet, artless girl,
    That all **thy** poets **have not flattered.**

———————

I have tried **for a week,** and vainly I seek
    Words of wisdom to write to you here;
So, wishing you life free from sorrow and strife,
    Nor wanting **in** friends and good cheer,
With health—perhaps wealth—
        Love better than self,
And Truth, far **the best,** to the **end;**
        Since content it maintains
        While existence remains,
I subscribe myself, **Truly, your** friend.

STRENGTH for to-day, in house and **home,**
　　To practice forbearance sweetly;
　　To scatter kind words and loving **deeds,**
　　Still trusting in God completely.

A **VOLUME** of this kind, **it is** supposable, will be more **or** less frequently referred **to, in** future years, to revive fading recollections and recall **pleasant** associations; and, therefore, though it is so easy to **moralize, it** seems eminently fitting that helpful suggestions should accompany familiar autographs.

Let me **say, then,** that while in your youth **a favorable** combination of circumstances permits **so** much **of** happiness, the conditions of its enjoyment **cannot always** remain as now.

As the responsibilities, at present borne for you, shall **come to rest** on **your own** shoulders, and the darker **shades of** life's **history are unfolded,** you will find the peace, which floweth like a river, only in **the** degree in which you resolutely perform every known duty; and, forgetting your own wants—whether fancied or real— devote your thoughts, as well as your energies, to making **the** society **in** which you move, happier for your being.

That you may indulge **in** no selfish ease; **but** bestow, as well as enjoy, a full share of the pleasures of time, and afterward receive a crown of glory, **is** the earnest wish of your friend—

I **WOULD that I could** express my mind
　　To you, dear friend, in scribbling some rhyme;
　　But **you** know my failing as well as I,
　　And you'd better get another to try.

THAT one who can **work** right on, quietly waiting for recognition, if it come: if not, **yet** right on, is the true nobleman.

DOST thou know, love, that thy smile
Makes the whole world bright for me?
    Just **as** sunrise pours a sudden
Purple glory on the sea.
    Ah! had I that power, ever
Should the world look bright to thee.

I KNOW not what to write about,
    So many themes are pressing;
All good enough in very truth,
    But quite unprepossessing:
Each moment of thy future life,
Live holy, whether maid or wife.

And let it be thy constant care,
    Midst earthly joy and sorrow,
By watchfulness and fervent prayer,
    Each this day and to-morrow,
To be prepared when Christ shall come,
His heaven to make thy final home.

OH, those eyes! so calm, serene—
Sweetest eyes were ever seen.
Will the woes of coming years
Ever shadow them **with** tears? ·
Shall my life the sunshine **own,**
That last night upon me shone,
When, beneath the summer skies,
Beamed on me those brown, brown eyes?

THESE little souvenirs possess not their greatest value when first written; but as time, with scythe in hand, passes along, and we are left standing, we are not the same, but these lines remain. Some, to cheer the saddened by awakening slumbering memories of better things; and others serving as guide-boards on the road to eternity.

AND thou, too, whosoe'er thou art,
   That readest this brief psalm,
As one by one thy hopes depart,
   Be resolute and calm.

O fear not in a world like this,
   And thou shalt know e're long—
Know how sublime a thing it is
   To suffer and be strong

PRESS on: our life is not a dream,
Though often such its mazes seem.
We were not born to live at ease—
Ourselves alone to aid and please
To each a daily task is given;
A labor that shall fit for heaven,
When duty calls, let love grow warm,
Amid the sunshine or the storm;
With faith, life's trials boldly breast
Then come a conquerer to thy rest

As you travel through life, scatter kind words and gentle deeds; in so doing, you will enrich your soul Withhold them, and it tends to poverty.

MAY your life be like the day—more beautiful in the evening; like the summer—aglow with promise; and, like the autumn, rich with the golden sheaves, where good works and deeds have ripened on the field.

LET the road be rough and dreary,
 And its end far out of sight;
Foot it bravely—strong or weary;—
 Trust in God, and do the right.

LIFE is but a day, at best,
Sprung from night, in darkness lost;
 Hope not sunshine every hour;
Fear not—clouds will always lower.

ALL the paths of faith, tho severed wide,
O'er which the feet of prayerful reverence pass
Meet at the gate of Paradise at last.

IF I wake, or if I sleep,
Still the memory I keep
Of the tender light that lies
In the depths of those brown eyes.

BE blessings scattered o'er thy way,
 My gladsome, joyous, laughing sprite;
Be thy whole life one summer's day
  Without the night.

On this **leaf, in memory prest,**
May my name forever **rest.**

On this page I'll write, simply to indite
My name as your friend.

MAY thy life happy be,
Is my dear wish for thee.

It never **pays to** fret and growl
   When fortune seems our foe,
The better bred will push ahead
   And strike the braver blow;
      For luck is work,
      And those who shirk
Should not lament their doom,
      But yield the play,
      And clear the way,
That better men have room.

DESIRE not **to live** long, but well;
How **long we live, not** years, but actions, **tell.**

MEANNESS shun, and all its train;
Goodness seek, **and** life is gain.

A BEAUTIFUL life ends not in **death.**

ROUND went the autograph; hither it **came,**
For me to write in; so here's my name.

PASSING through life's field of action,
   Lest we part before its end,
Take within your modest volume,
   This memento from a friend.

WE meet **and** part—the **world is wide;**
We journey **onward** side **by** side
A little while, and then again
Our paths diverge.   A little pain—
A silent **yearning** of the heart
For what **has grown of** life **a part;**
A shadow passing o'er the sun,
Then gone, and light again has come.
We meet and part, and then forget;
And life holds blessings for us yet.

WHEN things don't **go** to suit you,
   And the world seems upside down,
Don't waste your time in fretting,
   But drive away the frown.

OLD friends and true friends!
Don't talk to me of new friends;
      The old are the best,
      Who stand the test,
Who book their name as *through* friends.

MAY your coffee and slanders against you be ever the same—without grounds.

The world is full of fools.
　　And he who would none view,
Must shut himself in a cave,
　　And break his mirror, too.

METHINKS long years have flown,
　　And, sitting in her old arm-chair,
—— has older grown.
　　With silver sprinkled in her hair,
Her album thus she holds,
　　And turns its many pages o'er,
And wonders if it still contains
　　The memories of yore.
As o'er these pages thus she runs,
　　With many a sigh and kiss,
Then suddenly she stops and says,
　　"Who could have written this?"

IT never pays to wreck the health
　　In drudging after gain;
And he is sold who thinks that gold
　　The cheapest bought with pain.
　　　　An humble lot,
　　　　A cosey cot,
　　Have tempted even kings;
　　　　For station high,
　　　　That wealth will buy,
　　Not oft contentment brings.

REMEMBER me, is all I ask
And, if remembrance be a **task,**
  Forget me.

———

———, life is all before you,
  Stretched out in its misty sheen
And the future, though now hidden
  Holds much joy for thee, I ween
Why, then, seek to know what's coming
  It is forming day by day
But your heart, in blind out-reaching,
  Makes to-morrow of to-day.

"Life is real—life **is earnest:** '
  And the heroine **in the strife**
Is the one who leaves the future—
  Living **but the present** life ;—
Lives it truly, nobly, grandly
  Thus prepares for coming fate,
Strives to make her living perfect ;—
  Learns to labor and to **wait**

———

THE violet is for faithfulness,
  Which in me shall abide ;
Hoping, likewise, from your heart
  You will **not let it slide.**

———

THIS is thine album.   May it be
A **source** of happiness to thee.
And may each page that's written o'er,
Be better than the one before.

'Tis a terrible fate, my dear miss,
To be asked to write in a book like this;
For, scratch my head as hard as I may—
      I've such a skull—

And if I try to moralize,
   Or vent my thoughts in sentiment,
Or attempt to laud you to the skies,
   Or spread myself on compliment,
      I'm so awful dull,

That my efforts would prove futility;   [mind,
   For the sex of your kind, are of that turn of
That morals, verse and flattery,
   Have to you been so oft defined,
      You are full.

If rhyming I try, adorable Miss,
   The first I think of, is dear little Kiss,
Or some such nonsense as connubial bliss,
   Or changing your title "Mrs." from "Miss;"
      But that's prosaical.

To give you advice, I'd never presume;—
   Incompetence may be the reason for that ;—
To wish you long life and a blest happy home
   Is aged and stale, exhausted and flat,
      And excruciatingly formal.

Now, what to do I do not know,
   Or how to make my paragraph ;
So I'll doff my hat, and make my bow
   And send this as my autograph.

May there be just clouds enough o'er your life to cause
a glorious sunset.

THAT every kindly wish and thought,
  By friends expressed within these pages,
Be yours, and trials common to us all
  May cross your path by "easy stages."

REMEMBER me when far away,
  And only half awake ;
Remember me on your wedding-day,
  And send a slice of **cake.**

WHEN worth and beauty prompt **the line,**
Perhaps a pen as poor as mine
    May be forgiven
To try and write of things **divine,**
    And **think** of heaven !
But pause, rash verse ! and don't abuse
A bashful maiden's ear with news
    Of her own beauty !
And yet no other theme I'll **choose,**
    Or think a duty !
So, then, for fear I might offend,
I'll say, *God bless her !*—and thus end.

THE earth can boast no purer tie,
  No brighter, richer gem,
No jewel of a lovelier dye,
  Than Friendship's diadem.

Then may this ray of light **divine**
  Ne'er from our bosoms fade ;
But may it on our pathway shine,
  Till death our **hearts invade.**

———— is your name,
    Single is your station;
Happy be the little man
    That makes the alteration.

Oh love is **such a strange affair;**
So strange to all.
        It cometh from **above**
        And lighteth **like a dove**
                        On **some.**
        But **some** it never hits
        Unless it gives them fits.
                        Oh, **hum.**

T**HY** cheerful, gentle ways, I do admire;
Thy future, to be **happy,** I greatly desire;
Thy trusting **confidence,** may I require;
Thy firm friend to be, **will I aspire.**

As a slight token of esteem,
    Accept these **lines from** me;
So plain and simple, they do seem
    Unworthy such as thee.
But soon **these traced** lines will fade
    And disappear—'tis their **doom.**
May you, unlike them, **be arrayed**
    In a **perpetual bloom.**

I**N** memory's wreath may one bud be entwined for me.

WE are all placed here to do something. It is for *us*, and not **for** *others*, to find out what **that** something is, and then, with all the energy of which we are capable, honestly and prayerfully to be about our business.

On! think of me some day
When I am far away;
I'll pray thy days be long
And joyous as the song
Of sweet birds singing near,
Thy heart with love to cheer.

MAY joy thy spirit fill,
    All care and **sorrow cease**;
Remember 'tis His will
    Who hath spoken, "Peace!"

IN fair and sunny beauty, or gray 'neath evening **skies,**
The purple hills from misty vales, upward **to** heaven **rise:**
Their rugged side we scarce can see o'er-decked **with**
        fern and heather,
That rings its scented violet bells through **fair** and
         stormy weather;
So may thy life be clothed with flowers, **and breathe a**
        purer **air,**
Fresh from the "**everlasting** hills," knowing **no** grief or
        care,—
And if the sunny sky must **pale,** as pales the setting sun,
May it only show the **stars** are near, peeping out, one by
        one!

THESE **few** lines **to you are tendered,**
   By a **friend** sincere and **true;**
Hoping **but** to be remembered
   When I'm far away from you.

———

WORK, **while yet the** daylight shines,
   With **a loving heart and true,**
For golden years **are fleeting by,**
   And we are passing, **too.**

Wait not **for** to-morrow's sun
   To beam upon thy way,
For all **that thou can'st** call thine own,
   Is in **this** *one to-day.*

Then learn to make the most of life—
   Make glad each passing day—
For time **will** never bring thee back
   The chances swept away.

Leave **no** tender word **unsaid**—
   Do good while life shall last ;—
You know the mill can never grind
   With the *water that is past.*

Let not the hours **we've** spent together,
   Go past as nothing, **by ;**
Forget me not, e'en **though you must**
   Remember with **a sigh.**

———

THANKSGIVING-DAY again is here,
   And turkey is the leading **question ;**
I wish, with heartiness sincere,
   That **you** may have a good **digestion.**

Though many flowers have faded **from my life,**
 And clouds obscure the brightness **of its sky;**
This have I learned : **we can do much to make**
 Our lives a **blessing and our words a power,**
If **what we find to do, for Christ's dear** sake,
 We do with faithfulness, **from hour** to hour.

It may occur in after life
That you, I trust, a happy **wife,**
Will former happy hours retrace,
Recall each well-remembered **face.**
At such a moment I but ask—
I hope 'twill be a pleasant **task—**
That you'll **remember as a friend**
One who'll prove true e'en to the end.

I saw two clouds at morning,
 Tinged by the morning sun,
And in the dawn they floated on
 And mingled into **one;**
I thought that morning cloud was blest,
It moved so sweetly to the west.
Such be your gentle motion,
Till life's last pulse shall beat,
And you float on **in joy** to meet
A calmer **sea,** where storms **shall cease—**
A purer sky, **where all is peace.**

When on **this page you chance to** look,
Just **think of me** and close **the book.**

BE a good girl, and you will be a true woman.

MAY thy darkest hours in life be well lighted **with the** sunshine of contentment.

YOURS sincerely—although merely—

WHEN the golden **sun is** setting,
And your heart from care is **free,**
When o'er a thousand things you're **thinking,**
Will you sometimes think **of me ?**

How long we live, not years, **but** actions tell ;
That man lives **twice** who lives the first life well.
Make then, while yet ye may, **your God** your friend,
Whom Christians worship, **yet not** comprehend.
The trust that's given, guard ; and to yourself **be** just;
For, live we how we **can,** yet die we must.

LIVE well ; how long or short, permit to Heaven ;
They who forgive most, shall **be** most forgiven.

SOAR not too high to **fall,** but stoop to **rise ;**
We masters grow of all **that** we despise.

YOUR fate is but the common fate of all ;
Unmingled joys here to **no man** befall.

MISCELLANEOUS.

MAY e'en thy failings lean to **virtue's side.**

HOURS are golden links—God's token—
Reaching heaven, but one by one;
Take **them, lest** the chain **be** broken
Ere thy pilgrimage be done.

HOUSE beautiful—your book, from end to end,
And every page a room to lodge a friend;
Fain would I enter with a seemly grace,
Attired and mannered as befits the place;
But best endeavor falls below the aim
And rests at last, content to leave a **name.**

THE brave man **is not** he **who feels no fear,**
For that were stupid and irrational;
But, he whose noble soul its fear subdues,
And bravely dares the danger nature shrinks from.

FLING wide the portals of your heart!
Make it a temple set apart
From earthly use, for Heaven's employ—
Adorned with prayer and love and joy;
So shall your Sovereign enter in
And new and noble life begin.

WE could count time by heart-throbs; he most lives
who thinks most, speaks the noblest, acts the best.

WE ourselves shape the joys and fears
    Of which the life to come is made,
And fill our future atmosphere
    With sunshine or with shade.

WHEN the name that I write here is dim on the page,
And the leaves of your album are yellow with age,
Still think of me kindly, and do not forget
That, wherever I am, I remember you yet.

THE massive gates of circumstance
    Are turned upon the slightest hinge,
And thus some seeming pettiest chance,
    Oft gives to life its after tinge.

OH, for a home in Zululand, or Arctic regions cold,
A peasant's cot or hermit's hut, midst solitude untold,
With Kaffirs or with Hottentots, in Egypt or Leone—
'Twere bliss to live in *any* spot where albums are unknown.

IN times of prosperity our friends are many,
But the time of adversity tries and proves them

GEMS of price are deeply hidden,
   'Neath the rugged rocks concealed ;
What would ne'er come forth unbidden,
   To thy search may be revealed.

WHILE the fading flowers of pleasure,
   Spring spontaneous from the soil,
Thou wilt find the harvest's treasure
   Yields alone to patient toil.

IF recollections of friends brighten moments of sadness,
   What a fund of delight is here treasured for thee !
If advice and kind wishes bring goodness and gladness,
   How perfect and happy thy future must be.

THE tissues of the Life to be—
   We weave with colors all our own,
And in the field of Destiny,
   We reap as we have sown.

THERE is seldom a line of glory written upon earth's
face, but a line of suffering runs parallel with it; and
they that read the lustrous syllables of the one, and
stoop not to decipher the spotted and worn inscription of
the other, get the least half of the lesson that earth has to
give.

LEAF green on ground of white,
My name, I fain would write
That you remember still
In June or in December chill,
We two are friends.

———

On, wayward mortal who these books invented,
Why was't thou not by some kind hand prevented?
And thereby kept from many a luckless swain,
The direful knowledge that he lacked a brain—
Lacked it, at least, where poetry was needed,
Like the poor wight who here has not succeeded.

———

THROUGH days of doubt and darkness,
In fear and trembling breath,
Through mists of sin and sorrow,
In tears and grief and death;

Through days of light and gladness,
Through days of love and life,
Through smiles and joy and sunshine,
Through days with beauty rife;

The Lord of life and glory,
The King of earth and sea,
The Lord who guarded Israel;
Keep watch, sweet friend, o'er thee.

———

TRUTH—Freedom—Virtue—these have power:
If rightly cherished, to uphold, sustain,
And bless thy spirit, in its darkest hour.

Thy own trim, modest form,
   Is always neatly clad,
Thou surely will make the tidiest wife
   That ever husband had.

Among the many friends who claim
   A kind remembrance in thy heart,
I too, would add my simple name,
      Among the rest.

May **God's mercy** ever guide thee,
   Safe o'er all thy thorny road;
And His grace what'er betide **thee,**
Lead thee home to His abode.

The large are not the sweetest flowers;
The long are not the happiest hours;
Much talk doth **not** much friendship tell;
Few words are **best—I wish** you well.

Let your life be like **a snowflake,** which leaves a
mark, but not a stain.

Begirt with roses of **the royal June,**
A resurrected **day** swings highest morn
In every year; and so through life I pray
Nay **never failing** changes, bring their day,
And flames of love in swinging censers rise
While all thy thoughts leads on toward the skies.

SMALL service is true service while it last ;
  Of friends, however humble, scorn not one :
The daisy, by the shadow that it cast,
  Protects the lingering dew-drop from the sun.

MAKE good use of time, if thou lovest eternity ; yesterday cannot be recalled—to-morrow cannot be secured —to-day only is thine, which, if once lost, is lost forever.

IN time we transact business for eternity ; whatever, therefore, we do now, should be done well.

MAY each thought be pure, and sincere,
  Addressed upon these spotless pages ;
Reflections fond, they'll always prove,
  Youthful friend, through many ages.

THEY who have light in themselves, will not revolve as satellites.

THROUGH time we'll change, and then,
  This little book will somewhat bind us ·
You'll take it up, and think of me
  And all the joys we've left behind us.

As the shadow of the sun is largest when his beams are lowest, so we are always least when we make ourselves the greatest.

Across the page of spotless **white**
Friends trail the pen, and in our sight
Grow precious all the lines they write.

As for some white-sailed ship at sea,
So, little book, my watch for thee;
Return with freight of love to me.

EVERY hour comes to us charged **with** duty, and **the** moment it is past, returns **to** Heaven **to** register itself how spent.

THERE'S a Divinity that shapes **our ends,** Rough-hew **them how we** will.

OUR eyes see all around in gloom or glow,
Hues of their own, fresh borrowed from the heart.

WRITE your name by kindness, love and mercy upon **the hearts** of those you **come in contact** with, and you **will never** be forgotten.

LET Fate do her worst; there are relics of **joy,**
Bright dreams of the past, **she cannot destroy;**
They come in the night-time **of sorrow and care,**
And bring back **the** features that **joy used** to wear.
Like the vase, **in** which roses have once been distilled,
You may break—you may shatter the vase, if you will;
But the scent of the roses will hang round it still.

IF you wish success in life, make perseverance your bosom friend, experience your wise counsel, caution your elder brother, and hope your guardian genius.

COUNT that day lost whose low descending sun
Views from thy hand no worthy action done.

'TIS but a trifle that you ask,
  But this you will admit,
That trifles, more than greater tasks,
  Will sometimes strain our wit.
I wish thee health, and wealth, and joy,
  As others have before:
And were I in poetic mood,
  I'd surely wish thee more.

OUR greatest glory consists not in never falling, but in rising every time we fall.

HERE'S a sigh for those who love me,
  And a smile for those who hate,
And whatever sky's above me,
  Here's a heart for every fate.

IN all thy humors, whether grave or mellow,
Thou art such a touchy, testy, pleasant fellow;
Hast so much wit, and mirth, and spleen, about thee,
There is no living with thee, nor without thee.

MAY you live in bliss, from sorrow away,
Having plenty laid up for a rainy day;
And when you are ready to settle in life,
May you find a good husband and make a good wife.

I WRITE here a name which I hope shall be known
To all of the ages which follow my own.
'How conceited!' you say; but my lines shall remain;
'Tis my hope, you'll discover, not I, that is vain.

OUR lives are albums; each new day's a page
  As spotless as the leaf on which I write.
Whene'er those books of ours shall be read,
  May few unwise inscriptions meet the sight.

ON the broad highway of action
Friends of worth are far and few;
But when one has proved her friendship,
Cling to her who clings to you.

WERE mine the power I'd twine for thee
  A crown of jewels rare;
Each gem should be a kingdom,
  Each pearl an humble prayer.

THERE are few friends in this wide world
That love is fond and true;
But —— when you count them o'er
Place me among the few.

THERE is a small and simple flower
  That twines around the humblest cot,
And in the sad and lonely hours
  It whispers low : "Forget me not."

WHEN asked in an album to write,
  I feel quite inclined to refuse ;
For what should I dare to indite
  That would a young lady amuse ?
Not wit, for I have none of that,
  Nor romance—my fancy is tame ;
And compliments sound so flat,
  I'm forced to write merely my name.

MAY you always be happy,
  And live at your ease ;
Get a kind husband,
  And do as you please.

TRUE friends, like ivy and the wall,
Both stand together or together fall.

BEAUTY is but a vain, a fleeting good,
  A shining gloss that fadeth suddenly,
A flower that dies when almost in the bud,
  A bright glass that breaketh suddenly ;
A fleeting good, a glass, a gloss, a flower,
  Lost, faded, broken, dead within the hour.

MAY happiness ever be **thy lot,**
Wherever thou shalt be **;**
And **joy and pleasure** light **the spot**
That may be home to thee.

How sweet to have a faithful friend,
In whom we can confide :
To bless us if we act aright,
And if we err to chide.

HOPE the best, **get ready** for **the worst, and take what**
God sends.

BE content with the **lot God** has marked out for you.
Love, honor and obey Him **in** all things, and your last
days will be peaceful and happy.

MAY the morn of **thy life be bright and** joyous, the
noontide peaceful and happy, **and the sunset** gloriously
hopeful, is the wish of **your** friend.

LIFE, Death and Immortality—these three—the first,
the Road—the second, the Gate. **May** you walk safely
the first, pass triumphantly **the second, and rest** forever
in the third

MAY the Angels twine for thee
A wreath of immortality.

Yes, ——, I will write my name
  In here, as you request;
And, if to you its all the same,
I'll add a line—though rather tame—
  For Critics eyes, as my bequest.

My wishes and my hopes for you,
  Find glad expression here;
Although, indeed, its very true,
There is no room for all that's due
  To one we hold so dear.

Good health—first wish of all—
  Of all God's gifts the best;
A happy heart, that loves to call
On Him who notes the sparrow's fall
  And promises sweet rest.

Although beset by wordly care,
  Fix all your hopes on Heaven,
And view by faith the glories fair,
Which, in that world beyond the air,
  To faithful ones are given.

Although I am advised not to write fast,
I hope the thought I would express may last.

You ask for your Album a rhyme;
  With pleasure I hear and obey;
Refusal were folly or crime—
  For who could to —— say "nay?"

MAY Heaven on you its choicest blessings shower—
Is the sincere wish of your friend.

BE kind to all; be intimate with **few**;
And may the few be well chosen.

EVILS in the journey of life are like the hills which
alarm travelers upon their road; they both appear great
in the distance, but when we approach them, we find
them far less insurmountable than we had conceived.

MISS —— ! O Miss —— !
What can I write that's new
Among so very many
Pretty compliments to you?
In poetry, I fear I'd fail—
I'm very sure I'd stammer—
You cannot drive the ponderous nail
With a small ten-cent tack hammer.
Since, **then**, so high I cannot soar,
Nor chirp notes like the lark,
Please cancel what I've said before,
I'll simply make my mark.

IT has been **beautifully** said: The water that flows
from a spring does not congeal in winter; and those sen-
timents which flow from the heart cannot be chilled by
adversity.

Roses, without thorns, **for thee.**

I'll just write a few words here; so that when
You turn these and life's pages o'er again,
Your memory back to the time will go,
When you and I were "O" and "Jo."*

How we worked together in '79,
Wafting lightning over the W. U. Line
To W. M.—called "our quod," you know—
When you and I were "O" and Jo,

How Lu talked by the hour to us,
(And we stood it like martyr's making no fuss),
How we used to get "snatched"—we hated that so—
When you and I signed "O" and "Jo."

I'll not wish you all sunshine; for life is made
Up of installments of sunlight and shade.
May you never be worse off through life, as you go,
Than when on W. M. wire we signed "O" and "Jo."

May the hinges of our Friendship never rust.

May your days in joy be passed
With friends to bless and cheer,
And each year exceed the last
In all that earth holds dear.

---

* Initials used by telegraph operators.

There's many a trouble
Would break like a bubble,
And into the waters of Lethe depart,
Did not we rehearse it
And tenderly nurse it,
And give it a permanent place in the heart.
Resolve to be merry,
All worry to ferry,
Across the famed waters that bid us forget.
And no longer fearful,
But happy and cheerful,
We feel life has much that's worth living for yet.

May we always remain as good friends as we are neighbors.

The night has a thousand eyes;—
The day but one;
Yet the light of the whole world dies
With the setting sun.

The mind has a thousand eyes—
The day but one;
Yet the light of the whole world dies
When love is done.

On this spotless page my pen essays to trace a record of affection; and, as I write, a wish is in my heart that, for thee, every life-leaf will be written with the golden pen of love.

THOUGH many friends have signed their names,
   And some have left their mark,
I see a place for me remains
   To add my small remark.
My wish for thee is: joy through life;
   And bliss supreme, when some one's wife.

I PRAY the prayer of Plato old:
   God make thee beautiful within;
And let thine eye the good behold
   In everything, save sin.

A FEW true friends to aid us and love us,
   And cordial hands to warmly clasp our own;
O! surely God hath never made us
   To live distrustingly, selfish, and alone.

A VERSE you ask this fine day:
   Of course I'll write you one.
The task of writing finds its pay
   In joy that it is done.

WHY ask a name;
   Small is the good it brings;
Names are but breath—
   Deeds—deeds alone—are things.

WHEN years and months have glided by,
  And on this page you cast your eye,
Remember 'twas a friend sincere
  That left **this** kind remembrance **here.**
With best wishes for your future cheer.

DEAR ———, may your life be blest
With friendship, love and happiness;
May all your friends prove true,
And cheer you all the journey through.

MAY Future, **with her kindest smile,**
  Wreath **laurels for** thy brow;
May loving **angels** guard **and keep thee**
  Ever pure as thou art now.

IF writing in Albums remembrance **insures,**
With the greatest of pleasure **I'll** scribble in yours,

IN after years when you recall
  The days of pleasures past,
And think of joyous hours and **all**
  Have flown away so **fast,**
When some forgotten air you **hear**
  Bring back past scenes to thee,
And gently **claims** your listening ear
  Keep one kind thought for **me.**

THE truest happiness is found in making others happy.

ACCEPT my friend these lines from me,
They show that I remember thee,
And hope some thought they will retain
Till you and I shall meet again.

FOR thee, my fair and gentle friend,
I ask not wealth or fame,
I only ask thy path may be
Free from lifes toil and care.

AMONG the many friends that claim
A kind remembrance in thy breast,
I too would add my simple name.
Among the rest.

NEVER grow weary doing good.

I WANT a warm and faithful friend,
To cheer the adverse hour;
Who ne'er to flatter will descend,
Nor bend the knee to power;
A friend to chide me when I'm wrong;
My inmost soul to see;
And that my friendship prove as strong
For him as his for me.

⇢✢ ESTEEM and CONFIDENCE. ✢⇠

Some little token of regard,
 You wish from me to claim;
But as time is pressing hard,
 I will but write my name.

Every joy that heaven can send;
 Wealth, and every kind of treasure;—
Health and love to thee, my friend,
 And happiness without measure.

In future years, should trusted friends
 Depart like summer birds;
And all the comfort memory lends,
 Is false and honeyed words,
Turn then to me who fain would prove,
 However thy lot be cast,
That naught his heart can ever move
 From friendship of the past.

MAY your path be strewn with roses,
 Fair and flowery to the end;
And when your body in death reposes,
 May your Maker be your friend.

WELL, ———, I surely would like to please;
 But can't think what to say.
All your friends have wishes bright,
 To cheer your life so gay.

I will add: May all their words
 Be symbols of love and truth;
That when you grow weary, and seek for rest,
 You will rejoice in the friends of your youth.

To write in your Album, dear friend you ask;
Ah, well! it is not such a difficult task.
All I can say is contained here in one line:
May the blessings of Heaven forever be thine.

LET not our friendship be like the rose, to sever;
But, like the evergreen, may it last forever.

HE who does good to another, does also good to himself—not only in the act, but in the conciousness of well-
doing is his reward.

IN the evening of life, cherish the remembrance of one
who loved thee in its morning.

SPEAK of me kindly when life's dreams **are o'er ;**
Speak of me gently when I am no more.

SAFELY down Life's ebbing tide,
May **our** vessels smoothly glide,
And anchor side by side—in heaven.

THAT Hope and you,
Bright days will view.

GUARD well thy thoughts; our thoughts are heard in heaven.

MAY He who hath pencilled the leaves with beauty, given the flowers their bloom, and lent music to the lay of the timid bird, graciously remember thee in that day when He shall gather His jewels.

FROM memory's leaves,
I fondly squeeze
Three little words—
Forget Me Not.

A LONG life, and a happy one;
A tall man, and a jolly one—
Like—well—you know **who!**

THE hills are **shadows, and they flow**
   From form **to form, and nothing stands;**
They **melt like** mist, the solid lands,
   Like clouds they shape themselves and go

But in my spirit **will** I dwell,
   And dream my dream and hold it true;
For though **my pen doth** write adieu,
   I cannot say for aye farewell.

GOD's love and peace be with **thee, when**
Soe'r this soft Autumnal air
Lifts the dark tresses of thy hair.

Thou **lack'st not** friendship's spellword, nor
The half-unconcious power to draw
All hearts to thine by Love's sweet law.

With **such a** prayer, **on this sweet day,**
As thou mayest hear and I may say,
I greet thee, dearest, far away.

THIS Album's **a mansion which offers** its best,
   To the friends **who** have **written their** thoughts,
And the banquet is spread **with festal fare,**
   Where guests mingle enjoyment **with** rest;
And they leave their memorials under thy roof,
   Sometimes in sorrow, more **oft in joy** divine,
Nor think a single thought quite good enough,
   To measure **its faintest** pulse with thine.

→✶ BIRTHDAY VERSES. ✶←

I wish thee every blessing
  That can attend thee here;
And may each future birthday prove
  My wish to be sincere.

Your Birthday will always be green in the memory of your friends.

May these flowers, presented on your birthday, be emblematical of the purity of your life.

Wake early this morning,
  Nor miss the grey dawning;
Take this greeting from me
  As it goes straight to thee:
May joy and gladness e'er be thine;
  And endless brightness round thee shine.

49

This is thy Birthday, may it be,
A source of happiness to thee,
And may each Birthday yet in store,
Be brighter than the one before.

Dear friend, on this thy natal day,
I send to thee a little lay,
   And wishes tender
And only ask that thou'lt repay
My thoughts with thine, and fondly say,
   "I thank the sender."

May Spring its blossoms round thee strew,
And Summer, deck'd in mantle new,
   Come forth to greet thee;
May Autumn fruitage crown the year,
And Winter, with its jovial cheer,
   Bring friends to meet thee.

And if I still must absent be,
Do not forget to send to me
   One kind word only,
By home birds passing by the door,
Who, flying towards this distant shore,
   May greet me lonely.

Like sunbeams to the drooping flowers,
 Good-will our lives doth bless;
It furthers every wish of ours,
 And joys in our success.
So may its rays towards you flow,
 That none but friends your heart may know.

In these days of mirth and glee,
What shall my message be to thee?
What can I wish for one so blest?
Thou sunny bird in a sunny nest!
This I wish, and this I pray:
May the joys of life never pass away,
But only merge in a sigh of bliss—
Into a life far brighter than this!

If words could all my wishes say,
Oh! how my tongue would talk away.
I wish this day and many more
Might on dear ——— blessings pour.
May health, wealth, love, and peace
With each succeeding year increase;
And oh! the last, come when it may,
Be unto thee a happy day.

On this Birthday morn arise
From thy placid slumber!
Soon to meet love's longing eyes
And greetings without number.
Heavens dearest gifts be thine
To crown all earthly treasure,
For gifts that God gives unto thee
Know neither stint or measure.

As beauteous flowers in garlands intertwine,
May Peace and Love to cheer thy heart combine,
To give you a very happy Birthday.

LOVE in every bosom live,
And the truest pleasure give :
And happy smiles each lip adorn,
On this happy birthday morn.

LITTLE trouble and still less care,
With ever a faithful heart to share ;
Birthdays many, and happy too,
This is the life I wish for you.

DEAR, happy birthdays, how fair ye seem,
        Along the path of time :
Foot-prints whereon sweet-heart flowers blow,
        By worldly storms unriven,
That we may mark them as they go,
        And find our way to heaven.
BRIGHT as a flower may thy Birthday be.

TRUE love shall live thro' sorrow's wintry storm,
And bloom afresh on this glad Birthday morn.

LOVINGLY take this birthday souvenir,
And for my sake esteem it dear !

MAY the morning of thy birth break in gladness, and
the day teem with light-hearted mirth that shall last
always!

HUMOROUS.

I DIP my **pen** into the ink,
   And grasp your album tight;
But for my life I cannot think
   One single word to write.

IN the storms of life,
   When you need an umbrella,
May you have to uphold it
   A handsome young fellow.

MAY beauty and truth,
   Keep you in youth;
Green tea and sage,
   Preserve your old age.

SOME **people can be very funny;**
   I never could be so.
So I'll just inscribe my **name;**
   It's the funniest thing **I know.**

FEE SIMPLE and simple fee,
　　And all the fees entail
ARE nothing when compared to thee—
　　Thou best of fees—fe-male.

———

WHAT! write in your album, for critics to spy,
FOR the learned to laugh at?—No, not I!

———

ACCEPT my valued friendship,
　　And roll it up in cotton,
And think it not illusion,
　　Because so easily gotten.

———

WITHSOEVER is this for why?
Wherefore.　Ain't it?

———

WHEN I, poor elf, shall have vanished in vapor,
May still my memory live—on paper.

———

ROUND went the book, and here it came,
In it for me to write my name;
I would write better, if I could,
But nature said I never should.

———

IF you wish to laugh;
Glance at my autograph.

WHEN on this page you chance to look,
Think of me and close the book.

SAILING down the stream of life,
  In your little bark canoe,
May you have a pleasant trip,
  With just room enough for two.

DEAR FRIEND :—

Do not doubt me ;
You know more about me
Than many whose names
          Here appear.
But to tell them I'll never—
What ! never ? Hardly ever—
What I'd like to write to you
          Here.

'TIS nonsense I've written ;
You'll think I am smitten
With charms that I hold
          Very dear.
Please excuse me from writing,
More lines so inviting,
Your time to be spent
          Idly here.

I care not much for gold or land,
  Give me a mortgage here and there,
Some good bank stock—some note of hand,
  Or trifling railroad share,
I only ask that Fortune send
  A little more than I can spend.

MAN's love is like Scotch snuff—
You take a pinch and that's enough.
Profit by this sage advice,
When you fall in love, think twice.

LONG may you live,
Happy may you be,
When you get married
Come and see me.

MAY you be happy,
Each day of your life,
Get a good husband
And make a good wife.

As sure as comes your wedding day,
A broom to you I'll send ;
In *sunshine*, use the brushy part,
In *storm*, the other end.

I WRITE in your Album?
How very absurd!
My mind is at random—

MAY your cheeks retain their dimples,
May your heart be just as gay,
Until some manly voice shall whisper,
"Dearest, will you name the day?"

CHRISTMAS and NEW-YEAR

VERSES.

Joy and plenty in the cottage,
　Peace and feasting in the hall;
And the voices of the children
　Ring out clear above it all :
　　A merry Christmas!

As Christmas offerings meet your eyes,
Still closer be sweet friendship's ties.

Ring out, ye bells, o'er all the earth,
　To tell with brazen voice,
The tidings of the Saviour's birth
　And bid mankind rejoice.

True love shall live thro' sorrows wintry storm,
And bloom afresh on this glad Christmas morn.

57

OH joyous be your Christmas-tide,
  And bright your New Year, too;
To you may love ne'er be denied ;
  May all your friends be true.

OUR Saviour Christ was born
That we might have the Rose without the thorn.
  All through His desert life
  He felt the thorns of human sin and strife.
His blessed feet were bare
To every hurting brier.   He did not spare
  One bleeding footstep on the way
  He came to trace for us, until the day
The cruel crown was pressed upon the Brow
That smiles upon us from His glory now.

And so He won for us
Sweet, thornless, everlasting flowers thus.
  He bids our desert way
  Rejoice and blossom as the Rose to-day.
There is no hidden thorn
In His good gifts of grace.   He would adorn
  The lives that now are His alone,
  With brightness and beauty all his own.
Then praise the Lord who came on Christmas day
To give the Rose and take the thorns away.

AGAIN the festive season's here,
With all that can delight and cheer ;
Oh ! may you nothing lack each day,
But find fresh blessings strew your way.

Ring in, ring in the revelries,
　　And let the feast be one
Where **not** a single guest there is
　　But **Innocence** and Fun!
Let Christmas warmth keep winter out,
　　And joy unbroken reign—
From floor to roof-tree send the shout
　　Till Christmas comes again!

A LITTLE bird comes singing,
　　Singing a song to you;
He sings of sun tipped **flowers,**
　　Bathed in a diamond dew.
"The days are coming," **he** warbles,
　　" When the frost has flown away,
When the earth will be sweet with flowers
　　And the breath of new-mown hay."

Oh bird so softly singing
　　Your song of pleasant days,
Go sing to her I fondly love,
　　Through the wintry cold and bare.
When the heart is light, the days are bright,
　　And the sun seems ever near;
So sing her your lay this Christmas Day,
　　And through all the bright New Year.

On! may thy Christmas happy **be,**
　　And naught but joy appear,
Is now the wish I send to thee,
　　And all I love most dear.

Now Christmas comes with hearty cheer
   May kindly thoughts go round,
And bring to you a glad New Year,
   With peace and plenty crowned.

CHRISTMAS is coming, and what will it bring?
Many a pleasant and gladdening thing!
Meetings and greetings, and innocent mirth:
All that is brightest and best on the earth.

CHRISTMAS comes, let every heart
In Christmas customs bear its part:
The "old" be "young," the sad be gay,
And smiles chase every care away.

SURE, Christmas is a happy time
   In spite of wintry weather,
For laugh, and song, and jest go round
   When dear friends meet together:
And hearts are warm, and eyes beam bright.
In the ruddy glow of Christmas night!

FOR friends we strive to pierce
   The future, dense and dark,
But not a ray of light
   We see, nor faintest spark;
But yet while we have faith to cheer,
We trusting wish "A bright New Year."

HARK, the pearly air is trembling,
  Liquid music floats along;
Angels, in sweet joy assembling,
  Thrill the skies with heavenly song.
" Peace on Earth," is their refrain,
  Oh. be it yours this peace to gain.

MAY piety with wishes placed above,
And steady loyalty and faithful love,
Be thy blessings this Christmas-tide.

O LIFE is but a river
  And in our childhood we,
But a fair and running streamlet
  Adorned with flowers, see.

But as we grow more earnest,
  The river grows more deep,
And where we laughed in childhood,
  We, older, pause to weep.

Each Christmas as it passes,
  Some change to us doth bring,
Yet to our friends the closer,
  As time creeps on, we cling.

MAY health and joy, and peace be thine
  Upon this Christmas day,
And happy faces round thee shine
  As plenteous as the flowers in May.

O BRIGHT be the day
　Sweet echoes resounding,
Love lighting the way　·
　And warm hearts surrounding.
May the breath of His peace
　In thy spirit remain,
Till Christmas revisits
　The round world again !

———————

LET the New Year be to you
As a childish playmate new,
Stealing suddenly among
Apple-boughs that overhung.

Greet him half in confidence,
Half as ready for defence !
Is he come to tease or play ?
Will he give or take away ?

Let him come as friend or foe !
No New Year can overthrow
This our friendship that has grown
From the years that now are flown.

———————

O CHILDHOOD is a golden time,
　When all the world is bright,
When sunshine comes with every morn,
　Sweet dreams with every night.
Were I a fairy, I would give
　To thee a magic kiss,
That should ensure for the New Year,
　As fair a time as this.

TAKE, my friend, this heartfelt greeting,
Happy be thy Christmas day,
Faith, and hope, and love here meeting,
Speed thee on thy New Year's way!

I CANNOT tell what thou wilt bring to me,
O strange New Year,
But tho' thick darkness shrouds thy days and months
I will not fear.
Why should I fret my heart to know before
What may befall?
With this one thought content—I ask no more—
God knows it all.

HEALTH and prosperity
Your life to cheer,
With every blessing
For the bright New Year.

ON this New Year's morning
My wishes take their flight,
And wing to thee a greeting
That would make all things bright.

GLADLY now it is my pleasure,
Joys to wish you, without measure,
Happiness and peace attending,
With pure heavenly blessings blending.

MAY the blessings of the old year follow in the new.

WE cannot look into the future,
  We cannot tell if the New Year,
Will bring us fresh sorrows to mourn o'er,
  Or bring us new blessings to cheer.

But an all-seeing God is above us,
  Who knows what for each one is best,
Who in this world will care for and love us,
  And bring us at last to our rest.